simply
spooky

'brilliantly chosen by Wendy Cooling ... all are gripping, and offer real substance ... Each is a ray of sunshine for parents who are gloomy about the cost of encouraging their children to read. It's worth investing in the set.'

simply spooky

stories chosen by
Wendy Cooling

Dolphin

A Dolphin Paperback
First published in Great Britain in 1997
by Orion Children's Books
a division of the Orion Publishing Group Ltd
Orion House
5 Upper St Martin's Lane
London WC2H 9EA

A catalogue record for this book is available from
the British Library
Typeset by Deltatype Ltd, Birkenhead, Merseyside
Printed in Great Britain by Clays Ltd, St Ives plc

Contents

The Pirate Experience

Chris Powling

Griff realised this coastline was supposed to be haunted because it said so in the guidebook. Page after page told of smugglers, ship-wreckers and assorted fishing folk who were denied a proper burial, on land or at sea, because their bodies had never been found. 'This place is stiff with ... well, stiffs,' his dad had declared. 'Stiffs of the see-through persuasion.'

'You mean ... *ghosts?*' Griff asked.

'Ghosts, yes. And ghouls. Sea-ghouls, I suppose you might call them.'

His father began to squawk spookily, and flap his arms, to make sure Griff got the joke.

At the time it had seemed quite funny – even the lady who owned the hotel had laughed politely as she served their tea. Now, though, exploring the hotel grounds while Dad took his afternoon nap, Griff wasn't so sure. Okay, so he was still close enough to the main building to get help if he shouted loud enough. Okay, so he was prepared to admit he had the kind of imagination that was always on red alert. And okay, so this was the height of the holiday season ... three good reasons why he shouldn't panic at the sight of a pirate – an actual living and breathing pirate – sunning himself on the grassy mound up ahead. 'Er ... hello, Captain,' he managed to say.

'You all right, matey?' growled the pirate.

'I'm fine,' said Griff, faintly.

'So am I, more o' less, what's left o' me.'

To show what he meant, the pirate lifted the hook

he wore instead of a left hand and the wooden stump that replaced his left leg. His grin was so broad and so wolfish, Griff could have counted his teeth if he'd been able to tell which were gaps and which were just black.

Laboriously, with much grunting and groaning, the pirate clambered upright. Griff noticed he had an eye missing, too – or, at any rate, one that was covered by a black patch. It was his left eye. Somehow, this suited his left ear which clung to his head like a shrivelled leaf hardly able to bear the weight of its heavy, gold earring. 'Look at me starboard side,' the pirate advised. 'There's not a lot wrong with me starboard side.'

'Glad to hear it,' said Griff.

'What?'

'I mean … I like both your sides, actually. Honestly, I do. But it would be a bit much, I suppose, if *both* your legs were …'

'A bit much? It would be monstrous, matey, *monstrous*. I'd be tottering about like a couple of props in search of a clothes line. Thank God and all his angels I only got scuppered on me port side, that's what I say.'

'So do I,' said Griff, hastily. 'That's what I say, too.'

'You'd better, matey …'

The pirate tapped his nose with his hook.

Then, abruptly, he turned away.

Now he was staring out to sea – a perfect outline of a pirate (though hunched slightly to starboard) on the edge of a perfect cliff on a perfect midsummer day.

Griff seized his chance to review the situation. Being so dreamy and easily bored, he was the sort of person who could wallow in any fantasy if he was in the right mood – such as the flood they'd encountered yesterday when driving along the motorway. He'd been convinced it was more than the usual mirage. 'Of course it's a mirage,' his Dad had insisted. 'How could it be a flood when we're in the middle of a heatwave?'

'Well, it looks like a flood.'

'Griff, they always do. If it was a flood we'd be splashing through it sooner or later ... but we'll never catch up with this one, I bet you. It's just like a rainbow. However hard you try to steal up on it, somehow it's always the same distance ahead.'

'That's weird.'

'It's optical, Griff. Just an illusion that goes with weather like this. Basic physics, that's all.'

'If you say so, Dad.'

And Dad did say so, for the rest of the journey, practically, though in Griff's opinion a flood would have been much more fun.

Did the same basic physics apply to the sort of pirate mirage you can hear as well as see, though?

Cautiously, hardly daring to breathe, Griff looked the pirate over. He was standing absolutely still. Naturally, bits of him shifted in the sea-breeze – a flap on his three-cornered hat, for instance, or the tassels at the end of the sash he wore over his shoulder – but he gave no impression at all that if you tried to steal up on him, he'd always be the same distance ahead.

On the contrary, Griff was convinced you could get a great deal closer to this pirate than was good for your general health. Perhaps no one needed this much fun.

He began to back away.

Instantly, the pirate swung round. 'And where are you off to, matey?' he growled. 'Jumpin' ship already?'

'Who me?' Griff squeaked.

'Yes, you – you bein' the only crew on the quarter-deck apart from meself.'

The pirate leered at him with a horrible combination of patch and tooth and shrivelled ear.

Griff stayed right where he was. He felt a single bead of ice-cold sweat trickle centimetre-by-centimetre from the scruff of his neck, down between his shoulder-blades, as far as the small of his back.

Slowly, his one eye glinting at Griff in a speculative, was-this-a-case-for-keelhaulin' kind of way, the pirate began to tap his hook against the bare blade of the cutlass that slanted down the port side of his body.

Clink-clink-clink.

It was the scariest sound Griff had ever heard. 'Please,' he croaked. 'Please … I'm only a kid on holiday. We're staying at the hotel just through the trees. What's the point of skewering me?'

'Practice,' said the pirate flatly.

'Showing off, more like,' came a cool, crisp voice. 'Granpa, are you up to your old tricks again?'

Griff felt dizzy with relief.

He didn't even mind that the newcomer who'd come up behind him was a girl – a girl at least three or four years older than he was, he estimated, though it was hard to tell from her baggy shirt, canvas breeches and hair tied back into the sort of pigtail some boys wore nowadays. 'Are you a pirate, too?' he blurted out.

She grinned ruefully. 'Well, we'd certainly like you to think so – Granpa, especially. He used to be an actor, you see. Sometimes he forgets how convincing he is when he's playing a part.'

'Right,' said Griff.

'Did he really frighten you?'

'Just a bit ...'

'See, Granpa. I keep telling you, don't I? We'll never get any customers at this rate. Instead of attracting them, you're scaring them away.'

'Customers?' said Griff. 'What customers?'

It was the wrong thing to say.

The girl bit her lip and looked down at her bare, dusty feet. The pirate gave a shrug, swivelled on his stump and gazed out to sea again as if a horde of customers might appear over the horizon at any moment. 'Things will be ship-shape soon enough,' Griff heard him mutter. 'We just needs to bide our time till the tide turns an' that's a fact.'

'Granpa, we've been biding our time since the summer began and that's another fact. Also we were slogging away for most of the winter to make sure we were ready. How much longer have we got to wait before anyone signs up?'

'Signs up for what?' Griff asked.

'Don't you know? You haven't seen our adverts in the local paper, then? Or our posters stuck up all over the town? There should be one on the hotel notice-board, actually. I pinned it up myself so no one could miss it.'

Griff caught the dismay in her voice. 'Look,' he said quickly, 'we only got here a couple of hours ago. We haven't had a chance to look round yet, not properly. We haven't even unpacked.'

'Who's we? A coach party, is it?'

'Just me and my Dad, I'm afraid. We're ... we're not

sure how long we'll be stopping. We're touring, you
see. We book in at whatever place takes our fancy.
Then, if we find we like it, we stay put for a while.'

'Sounds nice.'

'It is,' said Griff. 'Well … sometimes it is. It can be
pretty tedious as well, to tell the truth. I bet it's nicer
being a pirate.'

'Pretending to be a pirate, you mean.'

'Sure.'

Griff nodded cheerfully.

Now he'd got used to them both, he could see how
far they were from being real buccaneers. The girl's
outfit didn't quite fit, for instance – as if it had been
nipped and tucked here and there to take account of
her girlishness. Even Granpa, who cut a much more
convincing figure, couldn't help looking a touch
theatrical when you came to examine him closely.
Why, anyone could have a face as weatherbeaten as his
with the clever application of greasepaint like the
sticks of Number Five and Number Nine Griff had used
in the school play last term. As for the wooden leg, a
neat bit of strapping up would create the space for that.

In short, they were good … but not that good.

Griff glanced back towards the hotel. What with the
brightness of the greenery in between and the shadows
creeping further and further over its stonework as the
afternoon advanced, the whole place had a blurred,
slightly hazy look as though it might fade away
altogether without intense concentration on his part.
He wouldn't have minded the same control over the
temperature. This seemed fiercer than ever. Much
more of it, he felt, and the world would be burnt to a

crisp by bedtime. 'Hey!' he said. 'Tell me about this poster of yours. What do your customers get for their money?'

'Doubloons,' Granpa snapped. 'Ducats and pieces-of-eight … if they're lucky. If they're not then it's buckets of blood!'

'Gramps, do leave off,' said the girl. 'It's a simple question needing a simple answer.'

She shook her head wearily. 'I still can't believe you haven't seen our poster. I shifted all the other notices on the board in the hotel lobby to give ours the prime position – so it would be the first thing every guest saw. What a waste of time that was!'

'Yes, but what does it say?'

'Oh … it announces "The Pirate Experience".'

'What?'

'THE PIRATE EXPERIENCE,' Granpa roared. 'Put your heart into it, girl. This is no time for the sort of lily-livered shilly-shallying you get from landlubbers! We've got an investment to protect.'

'We'll need a press-gang to do that!'

'A press-gang, eh …'

'Granpa, don't even think about it. It's called kid-napping nowadays and you go to prison for it. Besides, it's not even historically accurate. Plenty of pirates were refugees from press-gangs.'

'Maybe so, but –'

'Granpa!'

The pirate pulled a face, mostly to starboard, and held up his hand and his hook as a sign he'd struck his flag on the matter.

His granddaughter was quite right to keep him

firmly under her thumb, Griff decided. In a way, he was just like Dad – a big tease who never quite knew when to stop. Dad was an accountant in real life, though, not an actor. Investments were something he took very seriously.

On the other hand, so did this girl. There was a glint of real anger in her eye as she glared at her granpa. Embarrassed, Griff looked away. 'Why don't you bring me up to speed on this Pirate Experience?' he suggested. 'I mean, I reckon I've got the overall idea but what exactly does it amount to?'

'Would you like to see for yourself?'

'Now?'

'It'll only take a moment.'

'Walking a plank would be quicker,' added Granpa. 'But not by much.'

Griff shuffled his feet uncomfortably. 'Actually, I promised Dad I wouldn't leave the hotel grounds. It's not that I'm scared or anything – just that I don't want to break my word.'

'You won't be. The hotel grounds stretch right down to the beach and we won't be going nearly that far.'

'Oh … I see. I hadn't realised that.'

'Will you come, then?'

'Can't you just tell me about it? About the details on your poster, for instance? I really shouldn't be wasting your time.'

'Or *your* time,' sighed the girl. 'That's what you really mean, isn't it? Like all the other customers who haven't turned up all summer!'

Granpa gave a snort of disgust. 'Cast off, m'dear,' he scowled. 'This young whipper-snapper isn't worth it. If the cut of his jib is bein' marooned up here with his daddy, you're wastin' your breath tryin' to keep this conversation afloat.'

'Marooned?' said Griff. 'Who's marooned?'

He glanced at his watch. No problem there – assuming it really did take only a moment to see for himself.

He tossed his head to show them this wasn't a big deal for him one way or the other. 'Okay,' he agreed. 'But it had better not turn into a trek in heat like this. Sunstroke I can do without.'

The girl pulled her collar up over her neck. 'Me too,' she said. 'We can all do without that. Granpa, will you lead the way?'

'My pleasure, m'dear.'

'Tread carefully, then. That peg-leg of yours may be a fake but it can still topple you over easily enough.'

'You watch your step, m'dear, and I'll watch mine.'

And I'll watch mine most of all, Griff thought.

He was right about that. The cliff path was awkward as well as steep and he couldn't believe how well the old boy coped with it – hopping and skipping along the zigzagging track as nimbly as a mountain goat. Griff was still struggling to keep up when they rounded a jagged buttress of rock and saw, for the first time, the curve of the the bay below them. 'There,' said the girl, pointing.

'Ain't that a beauty?' Granpa remarked.

Griff simply stared.

Of course, they could have been referring to the view in general – the woods sweeping down to the shore, the frothy flop of the waves on smooth yellow sand, the sea itself as flat and clear and sky-reflecting as a mirror slotted into place between the jut of either headland. Griff knew what they were looking at, though. His eyes, like theirs, were fixed on the boat.

It wasn't big by any means. Was it a brig, or a ketch, or a schooner, Griff wondered? He hadn't the expertise to assign the right name to it, but he noted the trim of its reefed sails and the neatness of every other sea-going aspect, from stern to bowsprit, as if it had just finished preening itself – like a swan on a duckpond – to be certain of stealing the scene. 'Is that it?' he whispered. 'Is that The Pirate Experience?'

'Feast your eyes, matey,' Granpa advised. 'You'll not see a fairer sight 'cept if you sign on for a voyage. That's when we raise anchor, unfurl the skull-and-crossbones and slip away to where the treasure is ... buried beforehand, naturally, to spare the customers any disappointment. Now, is that favourite or what?'

'It's brilliant. Utterly brilliant.'

'You really think so?' asked the girl. 'Do you reckon your dad would approve of it?'

'I'll bring him here after supper,' Griff promised. 'It's not far to walk even for a lazybones like him. Maybe ... maybe we can be your first customers. Then we'll spread the word round the town till people are queueing along the beach to be the next ones aboard. You'll be digging up that treasure chest and covering it over again like a couple of good 'uns! Or a couple of bad 'uns, I should say. The Pirate Experience will be famous the length and breadth of this coastline!'

'Great!' the girl exclaimed.

' 'andsome,' echoed her granpa. 'And no more than we deserve, what's more, there's the rub of it.'

Griff couldn't disagree with that.

He was glad he'd said the right thing in the end. It meant they could wave each other goodbye with real cheerfulness. The last he saw of them was Granpa picking his way through the rocks at the water's edge towards a small, beached rowing-boat and the girl scurrying along in his wake, still telling him off no doubt, her pigtail bib-bobbing behind her.

The walk back to the hotel took him no time at all despite being mostly uphill. Soon he stood blinking in the sun-flooded lobby, not quite sure how to get his bearings again. Somewhere here, between the reception desk, the small forest of potted palms and the revolving doors of the entrance, was the place he was looking for. 'Where is it, though?' he asked himself.

'Where's what, young man?' someone asked.

Griff gave a start of surprise – more at himself for having spoken out loud than for not having seen her. The lady who owned the hotel peered at him curiously through the broad, shiny leaves she was cleaning. She was wearing a white apron now, with rubber gloves up to her elbows and a scarf to tie back her hair. 'I think your father's still upstairs, in his room,' she continued. 'If you've lost something, though, can I be of help?'

'The noticeboard,' said Griff. 'Where's the noticeboard? Wasn't it here earlier on?'

'It still is,' she smiled, 'but I lifted it down while I tidied the lobby. Look over there behind the reception desk. I'll hang it up again when I'm done. Did you have any particular notice in mind?'

'Only one,' said Griff. 'A special one. Probably you threw it away ages ago. It's a poster, actually.'

'Which poster is that?'

'For a boat trip ... called The Pirate Experience.'

He saw the smile fade slowly from her face.

Then, giving it her full attention, she began to scrub vigorously at a leaf she'd already polished. 'So you've heard about that, have you?' she said.

'I've heard something, yes.'

'You'll appreciate why nobody round here likes to talk about it, then. Tragic it was ... a pleasure-boat sunk overnight by a sudden, freak storm. By morning there wasn't a trace – nor of the old man and the teenage kid who were sleeping on board. He'd put his life savings into it, they say, and never saw a penny in return.'

She looked at him sharply. 'Not the sort of poster you forget to take down,' she said. 'In my hotel at any rate.'

'Of course not,' said Griff. 'I was only looking on the off chance. You see, something brought it to mind when I was out on my walk. And I wasn't sure when it actually happened.'

'This time last year ... to the very day, oddly enough. A day that was a lot like this one, come to think of it. It wouldn't surprise me if we don't get bad weather after dark tonight as well.'

'It does feel a big muggy,' Griff agreed.

He could see it, too, now he came to look. The white-painted walls of the lobby, still dazzling enough in the sunlight to make him screw up his eyes, had a hint – the merest coppery hint – of something meteorological in the offing.

Altogether, as Griff climbed the hotel staircase, he
was pretty certain he was in for another of Dad's
lectures on basic physics before he was very much
older. There was no way he could avoid it. He'd just
have to grit his teeth, he supposed, while Dad banged
on and on about the mechanics of thunder and
lightning and he did his best to bring the subject
round to mirages, and sea-ghouls, and what might be
included in the next, updated, version of the guidebook.

Garvey's Ghosts

Annie Dalton

The joke is, we only moved because of the ghosts. Mum and Dad had tried everything to get rid of them, calling in every expert going. From the New Age dowser who said our house was built over an underground stream, to a clergyman with staring eyes who put it down to having a disturbed teenager in the family.

'It's you that's crazy. My Lula wasn't more than *two* when these hauntings started,' our mum told him.

After that, Mum and Dad decided it would be safer for the Goodlucks to go it alone, so they sent me down to the Supernatural section of the library to pick up some hints. I could probably write my own ghost busting book now. Name a banishing technique: Tibetan bells, holy water, smudge-sticks, weird chanting, and I guarantee the Goodluck family tried it at least once.

It's not that these things didn't work. Everything worked. Even the Balinese wind-chimes. For a time.

But sooner or later, the hauntings always began again. Pictures crashing to the floor. Night-whisperings. Invisible skirts dragging their hems slowly down the hall . . .

This was the sixth house I'd lived in since I was a baby and every single one was as haunted as Hallowe'en. Maybe some families just attract ghosts, the way other people find coins in the gutter.

Anyway, one day I found Mum sweeping up bits of shattered picture frame for the zillionth time and she had a dangerous look in her eye. 'That's it, Garvey,' she declared. 'We're moving, only this time *I* decide where.'

It wasn't just the ghosts. Mum was always trying to get Dad to shift. 'It's time the Goodlucks moved up in the world,' she said.

'Mum, this is our home, not Snakes and Ladders,' I began.

But Mum was punching microwave buttons. Mum never listened to me anyway. She didn't listen to Dad when he got home, either.

'We've only just got this house straight,' he said unhappily.

'Straight!' echoed Mum. She pointed at Gran's photograph tilting ominously on the wall. 'Is that what you call it?'

'I love our house,' snuffled Gracie, clutching Banoffee. Gracie always drags our cat round with her like a furry comfort blanket.

'You'll love the new one too, sweet pea,' said Mum. 'I promise.'

'You're wrong there, Mum,' I said, but I was careful to say it under my breath.

Dad just stared blankly at his plate of microwaved korma. Dad's like me, the strong silent type. Well, silent anyway.

Sometimes I felt a bit like a ghost myself.

When moving day came and we drove away from our tatty old house, with Banoffee yodelling furiously in the back, my heart dropped deep into my boots.

'Missing your spooks already?' whispered Lula.

....

It was true. After eleven years I'd grown used to the steady shimmer of supernatural goings-on. Ghosts are confusing to have around, scary even, but to me being haunted was, well, normal. A world without that shimmer would be like a planet without oxygen.

As we drove into the estate I could feel my lungs starting to shrivel like tired balloons. I know new estates are incredibly clean and everything but so is the moon and you can't breathe there either. We drove past instant gardens and toy-town trees. We drove along a maze of empty sunlit streets with fake-poetic names. Khubla Khan Way, I ask you.

Our house was in Shangri La Close. Number 9.

Lula stared. 'Oh, goody, it's the gingerbread house,' she said insincerely.

We stood around waiting for Mum to do the honours.

'It used to be the show-house,' Mum carolled. 'It's so-o clean.'

'And so-o phony,' I said, but very softly.

'Strange,' Dad said, puzzled. He peered through the glass porthole into the hall where a rosy light shone warmly, as though to welcome us.

'The estate agents left it on to fool burglars,' said Mum firmly.

'They left the radio playing too,' Lula said. 'What a cool station.' She dipped and swayed dreamily.

'You're hearing things, Lula,' said Mum. 'The only sound in this street is the uplifting sound of birdsong. I'm going to sleep so well in this house!'

She turned the key with a flourish.

'Well, everyone,' announced Gracie brightly. 'At least a new house could *never* ever be haunted!'

Mum opened the door. 'You see,' she said, snapping off the light. 'What's supernatural about that? I want this family to understand that all that spirit-world business is behind us now. I've got nothing against disincarnate beings but we have our place in Creation and they have theirs. From now on, that's the way it's going to stay.'

Mum was right.

For almost twelve hours.

It was Gracie who woke me; stumbling in, bug-eyed with tiredness.

'That party is keeping me awake,' she whined.

'You're dreaming, Gracie.' I told her. 'There's no party.'

'Yes, there is,' Lula stood in the doorway. 'A ghost party.'

A *ghost party*? None of our previous ghosts had been the partying kind.

'There's no ghosts here, Lula,' I said uncertainly. '*Are* there?'

Lula shook her head. 'How do the Goodlucks do it?' she said. 'Just home-in on the unquiet dead every time. And I mean "unquiet".'

By the time I got to the landing the beat was pounding up through the ceiling into my bare feet.

'Does Dad's old stereo actually play that loud?' I asked, impressed.

Lula ignored me. 'That's my CD,' she said. 'They're mad about it. Don't you want to meet them, Gee? Our show-house spooks?'

'*Meet* them?'

'Yeah – they're a bit blurry round the edges, but they're visible all right. One looks Gracie's age, but she's probably older. Children were smaller in those days. Anyway, what's age, when you've been dead as long as these kids?' Lula was talking to herself.

'Ghost kids?' I said. 'You've been talking to ghost kids?'

'Yes,' said Lula in her dreamy voice. 'As much as you can with this row. They've been lost in the spirit world for so long they can't remember who they were. They kept finding themselves in horrible haunted houses full of fogey old spirits wringing their hands. They wanted a nice ordinary home, same as live people have. So they borrowed this one. They *love* the nineties, Gee. They love TV game shows and rave music and rap ...'

It was impossible to hear her now over the bass line. I flung open the living-room door. But even a lifetime of heavy-duty haunting couldn't prepare me for what was on the other side.

It's one thing to sense presences, or hear ghostly whispers in your ear. But to see wild-eyed ghost children whooping it up in a show-house, to your sister's new CD. *That*'s something else.

I shut the door quickly. 'What will we do, Lu?'

But Lula was in a crumpled heap, crying on the stairs. Seeing my big sister in tears was the scariest thing of all.

'Here, hold Banoffee,' offered Gracie. 'She always makes me feel better.'

Lula snivelled into Banoffee's neck for a minute.

Then she said hopelessly, 'Mum will go mental. She'll make us move again. I can't stand it. She mustn't find out. But you'll have to get rid of them, Gee. Because I just can't.' And she lay her head down on our long-suffering cat and howled.

Grace's lip started to tremble. 'The poor little lost children.'

'They aren't *dancing* like little children,' I said. But I felt lousy too.

'They only want some fun,' wept Lula. 'And real home cooking. They really miss food.'

Perhaps if you're silent long enough, the strength part eventually kicks in, like Popeye's spinach. Or maybe I'd just never *had* to be a strong person before. But suddenly, in an electrifying flash, I knew what to do.

'No more exorcisms,' I said in a surprisingly clear voice. 'And no more moving either. The ghost kids stay and so do we. So long as they fade into the background when Mum and Dad are around, the rest of the time we'll be, well, kind of adopted brothers and sisters.'

'But suppose Mum finds out,' wailed Lula.

'We'll handle Mum,' I said confidently. 'She's nuts about this horrible house. She'd rather be brained by the occasional falling picture than ever move again. But ...' I paused.

'But?' said Lula.

'We'll have to negotiate. If these kids want rights, they have to accept responsibilities too.' I was enjoying myself.

I flung open the living room door again. Three wild-eyed ghost children tumbled backwards.

'Did you hear all that?' I asked.

They nodded warily.

The tallest spirit had snaky hair and a rebel look. He stuck his thumbs in his waistband. 'We heard you, Garvey,' he said grinning. 'Rights and responsibilities, wasn't it?'

Lula bit back a tiny smile.

Gracie slid round me and stood in front of the littlest ghost. 'What's your name?' she said.

'Don't remember,' said the baby ghost, sticking out her lip as if she might cry. She yanked up her raggedy hem, flashing ghostly little chicken bone knees, and began sucking it furiously.

'Don't be sad,' said Gracie. 'I'll give you a new name. You can be Mo, okay? Do you like that name?'

'Who am I, Garvey?' said a husky voice. The third ghost had a sharp-faced streetwise look. Her tangled hair didn't quite hide the longing in her eyes.

I didn't hesitate. 'You're Harley,' I said. 'That tough enough for you?'

The ghost girl grinned with surprise. 'Almost,' she agreed gruffly.

'I hope you know what you're doing, Gee,' said Lula as we tucked Gracie into bed later.

'I do,' I said. 'Those kids have been blamed and blessed and banished for – for aeons now.'

'*Aeons*?' echoed Lula blankly.

'Since forever,' I said impatiently. 'I bet it was grim enough when they were alive. That's probably why they don't remember much. They need to be listened to for once. Appreciated. They need security. Then maybe, in a while, they'll move onward and upward, or whatever ghosts do. They need us, Lula,' I said.

And then the weirdest time of our lives began.

Don't ask what my new school was like, the day was just a blur of posh blazers and strange corridors.

When I got home, Lula was flicking through magazines. 'I've got a pattern for that jacket,' she was saying.

'Could it be exactly like the photograph, but leather?' Harley said excitedly. 'No wait, denim. Distressed denim.'

Mo was snuggled on the sofa with a blissful Banoffee, watching TV. Oprah was explaining how children need self-esteem to thrive. The snake-haired boy grinned, tapped his jangling headphones and stuck up his thumb.

Gracie lay on the rug, colouring. 'It's easy peasy, you stay inside the lines, see,' she told Mo. 'You do the next one, all right?'

'What's everyone up to?' I asked dazed.

'They need new clothes,' said Lula.

'We've been wearing this graveyard tat for *aeons*,' said Harley. She flashed me a wicked grin under her knotted hair.

'And it's not helping their self-esteem,' said Gracie.

'Harley wants this funky jacket,' said Lula. 'And Mo is going to have a sweet little ...'

'Hold on,' I interrupted her. 'How are you going to make clothes for them, Lula? You're alive. You're solid. They're ...'

'Not,' the snake-haired boy chipped in. 'I think Lula understands that, Gee.'

'Harley explained it to me,' said Lula. 'In the spirit

world when you want something, you just imagine it vividly enough and in enough detail and it just – *manifests* in energy form? Is that the word, Rain?'

Snake-hair nodded.

Rain? I thought. What kind of name is that?

'Manifesting is just like playing pretend, all right Garvey?' explained Gracie, still crayoning.

'Thank you,' I said weakly.

'But obviously their fashion ideas are incredibly out of date,' Lula went on. 'So I'm bringing them into the nineties.'

I think I was half-relieved to hear Mum's key in the door then.

'Vanish, you lot,' I ordered. 'That was our deal, remember?'

'How could we forget?' mocked Snake-hair.

They vanished. Except for Snake-hair's grin which hung smirking in the air until my giggling sisters swatted it with tea-towels.

'Why did you call him Rain?' I asked Lula as we cleared the table.

'Rain named himself actually,' said Lula, tossing her hair a bit. 'I think it really suits him.'

Mum was in the kitchen puncturing clingfilm. 'It's wonderful to be back,' she sighed, shoving the first batch in the microwave. 'I can't *wait* till I'm home all day long.'

The machine beeped. Mum shoved a blistering hot plate in my hands. I tried not to inhale its fake curry smell, glanced up and froze.

Hanging like a bat from our shiny new banisters was Rain, his grinning head dangling directly over our dining table. I made frantic cutting movements across my throat. 'You promised,' I hissed.

Lula quickly blocked Mum's view. 'So why will you be home all day, Mum?' she asked innocently.

'And you promised us food. But she's cooking horrible little boxes,' Rain hissed back. 'Food means real meat, real gravy, real sticky toffee pudding, Gee.'

'When the baby comes,' said Mum calmly.

Mum really picks her moments. We stared, speechless.

The microwave beeped. But I got there first.

'Don't let's eat this stuff, Mum,' I said cunningly. 'Let me and Lula cook tonight, to celebrate.'

So Lula and I cooked. And now and then while we chopped, stirred or threw more seasoning in the pot, I'd catch glimpses of the three ghost kids, dangling over our banisters, sniffing rapturously.

'You'd think it would torture them,' I whispered.

But Lula insisted *smelling* food was as good as eating to Rain and the others. 'They're in heaven,' she said.

And to judge from Dad's face when Lula sat him down at the table, he thought he was in heaven too.

Mum laughed. 'Now your Dad will want real food every day.'

'That's lucky,' I said daringly. 'It's Dad's turn tomorrow.'

'Your father!' Mum held her sides. 'He can't boil water.'

'I'll take that as a challenge,' grinned Dad. '*Chilli con carne* tomorrow, everyone?'

Things were turning out better than I thought.

There were tricky moments. Like when Gracie

smuggled Mo into nursery school, and the teacher complained Gracie spent more time chatting to her 'imaginary friend' than to her classmates. But generally our two families, the ghostly family and the living one, lived in harmony. We kept our side of the house-share deal. They kept theirs.

It was fun. The most I'd ever had. One night we played with Lula's karaoke machine and Rain did such a wicked impression of Michael Jackson I was in danger of dying young myself from laughing. Afterwards Rain taught us a tune of his own. And it was good; it was all right.

Next day, I heard Mum humming something that sounded just like Rain's funny little song. She seemed happy. Really happy.

All of us were happy. At least I thought we were.

Until the night Lula woke me by dripping her tears all over my face.

'It's getting out of control, Garvey,' she wept. 'I'm tired. I'm tired all the time. I never get a minute by myself. There's always someone reading my magazines, listening to loud music. If I try to watch a video, Harley wants to watch *Blind Date* instead. They keep on at me to design them new clothes. I'm behind at school. Then when I come home I have to cook the tea. To keep a deal you made, Garvey, by the way. And finally,' Lula was working herself up to a wail, 'I *hate* taking my clothes off, even alone in my room, because I never know if *someone* might still be there!'

She was pulling the weirdest faces. Finally I caught on. 'But I thought you liked Rain,' I said.

Lula flushed to the tips of her ears. 'That's not the *point*, Gee!'

Gracie stumbled in. 'Mo's taking up all the bed again,' she groaned.

'Lula says they've got to go,' I told her.

Gracie looked shocked. 'Not that starey old vicar, Garvey?'

I shook my head. 'No more exorcisms and no more house moves. I told you before.'

Lula slumped to the floor. For the first time I saw shadows under her eyes. 'What options does that leave?' She yawned.

'Cunning,' I told her. 'That's what. The ghost kids say they love the nineties but they haven't even *seen* the nineties yet, except on telly. We'll broaden their horizons. Help them manifest ghost plane tickets for a round the world trip, same way you did the clothes.'

'They'll need other stuff,' said Gracie. 'Sunhats, swimsuits.'

'Passports, sunblock,' said Lula. Her eyes gleamed. 'A luxury holiday,' she murmured. 'But will they go for it, Garvey? And if they do, will they *stay* gone?'

'Come on, Lu,' I said. 'Would you come back to Shangri La Close, if you had a choice?'

Our taxi driver couldn't get the hang of it.

'So I'm driving the three of you to the airport but you're not meeting anybody there and none of you is actually getting on a plane? Then I drive you home again?'

'I know it sounds peculiar,' said Lula sweetly. 'But

sometimes it's the only way we can get our little sister to sleep.'

In the end, there was no time for goodbyes. I think they were too excited. I'd hardly got the passenger door opened when something streamed past me into the parking bay, knocking me back in my seat. It was like being hit by three exuberant sea breezes all at once and I gasped. Lula and Gracie shut their eyes tight for a second, so I know they felt it too.

I'm almost certain it was Harley I saw, seconds later, towing skinny little Mo towards the check-in desk. She had a jacket like Harley's anyway. And the boy with her had snaky hair and a rebel look. I imagined Mo saying, 'Isn't New York where Oprah lives?'

The three of us waved madly at the first plane we saw boost itself into the sky, in case they were on that one.

'Onward and upward, kids,' I whispered. Then we climbed back in the taxi. 'It's over,' I said. And Lula and Gracie burst into tears.

I felt a bit choked myself.

The Goodlucks have been ghost-free for over a year now. Though Gracie still sleeps scrunched up at one end of her bed in case Mo comes back suddenly in the night. Banoffee yowled tragically round the house for weeks but baby Delia cheered her up a bit. (Another girl, wouldn't you know?) But there's something missing. That shimmer, that supernatural oxygen. It's not there.

That's why I brought Miles home for tea. I thought it was time I did something normal. But on the way home Miles kept saying, 'Haven't you got any Sega games?' 'Haven't you got *Mortal Kombat*?' Till I wanted to kick him hard. Then outside our door, Miles had the nerve to say, 'Don't you have anything interesting at your house, Goodluck?'

That's when I cracked. 'Well, Miles,' I said. 'We used to have some interesting ghosts. They thought they were tough little gangsters but they were soft as butter really. What they really liked was watching *Blind Date* and cuddling our cat.'

It was a strange moment. I waited to see what would happen next.

Miles stared, trying to figure me out, breathing noisily. 'You liar, Goodluck,' he said at last.

But then he started grinning. He thumped my shoulder, gurgling with genuine laughter now. 'You madman!'

I'd done the right thing! I was so surprised I grinned back. 'Got you going, eh,' I said in a just-kidding tone. Then I said, 'You can have a go with Lula's karaoke machine, though, if you want.'

'Karaoke, *wicked*,' said Miles, cheering up no end.

And we walked through the door of 9, Shangri La Close into the good smell of Mum's stew and the sound of baby Delia bashing her high-chair with a spoon.

Advice from a Dead Man

Alan Gibbons

Thinking back, I suppose I've always been a bit of a lone wolf. Mum says it might have something to do with being an only child. Or maybe it was down to being in a family of just the two of us. I don't know. Maybe it's just the way I am. So I suppose it's weird how much I came to depend on a complete stranger, especially when you consider that he was a dead man.

I met Jimmy Feeney one winter's evening at my local swimming pool. It isn't much to write home about, a draughty, vandalised shed of a building with half the window panes hanging loose against the security grilles like the loosened teeth of a boxer who's seen better days. But it does have a heated pool and I just love to swim. It kind of calms me down after another day being baited by the bullies at school. What is it with me, I always ask myself. Do I have victim pencilled on my forehead, or something? Still, it's my favourite part of the day. Since I was eleven Mum has let me go to the baths by myself. It was a battle at first. She'd wrap me in cotton wool if she could. But I finally won her over. It's only ten minutes from school and a leisure pass is cheap, so I go along most days. I have done for the best part of two years now. School is bad news and I'm a bit short on friends, so it does me good.

'Something wrong, son?' came Jimmy's voice as I clung to the metal rail at the poolside.

'No, nothing,' I told him.

I was lying. It had happened the day before, you see.
One minute I was walking down the back alley off the
main road, the next I was coming to on the floor. I'd
just blacked out. No warning or anything. I was scared,
I don't mind telling you. And tired. So tired I could
hardly struggle to my feet. Even that wasn't the worst
of it. What if Mum found out? She'd never let me out
of the house by myself again.

'The name's Jimmy Feeney,' Jimmy said. 'You sure
you're okay?'

'Sure I'm sure.'

I really snapped at the old guy. What gave him the
right to interrogate me? Anyway, I got away sharpish
and swam half-a-dozen lengths. When I glided back to
the side for a breather, he was still there. I remember
wondering why he wasn't with the rest of the grey
brigade. That's what the kids call the pensioners who
come along for a swim. They more or less take over the
pool. I've never noticed them doing that much swimming, though. They hang around together, getting in
the way. And they sing. That's right, sing. All these old
songs like *My Way* and *When I Fall in Love*. Then they
laugh and applaud themselves. Not Jimmy though. I'd
noticed him before. He was a regular. But he just swam
up and down on his own, and he never once spoke to
anyone else. Until the day he spoke to me that is.

'Well, I reckon something's troubling you,' he said.
'And I'm a good judge of character.'

'Not this time,' I retorted. 'I'm fine.'

And that was that. I hauled myself out of the pool
and went for a shower. As I got dressed I found myself
staring at my reflection in the mirror by the door. How

did he know I was worried? Did it show? Mum hadn't noticed, so why should he? I searched for his grey head ploughing through the water but he must have got out soon after me. I shrugged my shoulders and forgot all about it.

It was the end of the week before I went swimming again. I'd had a rough day and I took it out on everything I touched. If I couldn't thump the bullies at school, then I'd have to do it with whatever came to hand. I crashed through the door, slamming my fist into the first few locker doors as I stalked towards the cubicles.

'Something eating you, son?' came a familiar voice. It was Jimmy.

'Don't ask,' I said.

I noticed one of the lifeguards giving me a funny look, but I didn't give it a moment's thought. Some of them aren't keen on kids. They get too much lip off the scallies.

'I've got to get changed,' I told Jimmy. 'See you in a minute.'

The lifeguard was still staring. Really staring, like I was having a conversation with a giant mouse or something. What *was* his problem?

By the time I came out of the cubicle, Jimmy had vanished. I scanned every lane of the pool but there was no sign.

'Have you seen the old guy I was talking to?' I asked the nosy lifeguard.

He just looked down his nose at me. 'Who do you mean?'

'Big fellow,' I told him. 'He was right here. He shouted to me when I came in. You were watching us.'

The lifeguard squinted. 'Are you trying to wind me up?'

'Of course not.'

'Well, I didn't see any old guy,' he said grumpily.

Takes all sorts, I thought. And that's when I heard Jimmy calling to me from the pool.

'In you get, lad,' he shouted. 'Swim a few lengths. Nothing like it for easing away your troubles.'

I dropped into the pool feet first and bobbed back to the surface, squeezing the water from my eyes.

'Been swimming here long?' I asked.

'Since 1921,' Jimmy answered.

I gave a low whistle. 'I never knew it had been open that long.'

'Built in 1890, this place,' said Jimmy. 'There was an outdoor pool when I started coming. No heating, either.'

'It must have been freezing,' I said.

Jimmy's eyes twinkled. 'Oh aye, you had to be hard in those days. None of your central heating malarkey back then.'

'Yeah yeah,' I said sarcastically. 'Next you'll be telling me you could buy a Porsche and a Rolls Royce and still have change from a fiver.'

Jimmy just chuckled. 'You don't know you're born, son.'

It was about then that I noticed the lifeguard again. He'd taken his place on this high seat they have for observation. He wasn't paying much attention to anybody else, though. His eyes were fixed on me. It was making me uncomfortable.

'Do you think he's got a problem?' I asked Jimmy.

Jimmy glanced in the lifeguard's direction, then smiled. Without another word he swam off, doing a strong, easy crawl. I tried to follow him, but there was no catching him. He couldn't half shift when he wanted to. It was only as I was labouring down the pool in his wake that this idea popped into my head. 1921, he'd said. He started swimming here in *1921*. But that would put him in his eighties. If he'd said he was sixty I would have believed him. But eighty or ninety – no way. He was having me on. Either that, or he'd discovered the secret of eternal youth.

'I'm going to challenge him,' I told myself out loud.

But I didn't. He'd done his vanishing act again.

'Jimmy,' I said.

'Hello there, lad,' he said, the leathery-looking skin round his eyes wrinkling with pleasure. 'In a better mood today?'

I nodded. In the three days that had passed since our last meeting, I'd been pretty much left alone by my tormentors at school. What's more, my blackout was a distant memory. It was nothing, after all.

'Some of the kids have been getting on my back,' I explained. 'But they've gone a bit easier lately.'

'You've got to stick up for yourself,' said Jimmy. 'Even if they're bigger than you. Don't take it off anybody. I was a skinny little lad myself.'

'Never!' I stared at the slabs of muscle on his broad chest and the biceps on his arms.

'I was, but I didn't take any stick from anybody. Fought my way up. There's many a time the teachers put me in the ring with another lad for fighting.'

'You mean they made you box?'

'If you had a fight, they did. That was the way they sorted a scrap out in the old days.'

'It doesn't sound very fair,' I said. 'What if the bully won?'

'Who said anything about fair?' said Jimmy. 'It helped me, though. When I went working down the docks I had a good pair of fists. Made a man of me.'

'And when was this?' I'd just remembered my doubts about his age.

'Back in the twenties', he answered.

'So that makes you ...?'

'Sixty-five.'

I frowned. 'You can't be. What year were you born?'

'1901. The year old Queen Victoria died.'

I laughed, but Jimmy didn't see the joke. 'But you'd be nearly a hundred.'

It was Jimmy's turn to laugh. 'I don't know what they teach you in school today,' he said, shaking his head. 'But it isn't maths, that's for sure.'

With that he swam away, kicking hard with his legs. The chlorined spray hurt my eyes. By the time I'd cleared them he was gone.

The nightmare returned that evening. I was cycling home down Haddon Hill when it happened. Just like the first time. No build-up, no warning, just the sudden blackout. And when I woke up I was so tired I could barely put one foot in front of the other. Mum was worried sick when I finally got home. I couldn't tell her though. I was scared. I mean, what if I was dying? Besides, if I told her what had really happened, I could say goodbye to the little bit of freedom I had. In the end I told her it was a flu bug and turned in.

It was a few days before I went back to the pool. I'd been making excuses for days. I told Mum I was still under the weather, but that wasn't it. I was scared. What if I blacked out when I was swimming? I turned it over and over in my mind. Maybe I ought to tell Mum after all. I didn't, of course. My freedom was worth the risks. So there I was that Thursday evening, standing by the poolside, trying to pluck up the courage to take the plunge.

'Hello stranger,' came a familiar voice.

'Jimmy.'

'Got it in one, son.'

I slid into the water next to him.

'Do you come every day?' I asked.

'You could say I live here,' he answered.

I must have frowned, because he immediately added: 'Just a joke.'

The nosy lifeguard was hosing down the tiled poolside so for once I could talk to Jimmy without feeling his eyes on me.

'What's the matter?' Jimmy asked. 'You look like you've got all the worries of the world on your shoulders.'

'I'm okay.'   .

He didn't say a word in reply, but the way he looked into my eyes told me he didn't believe me.

'I am,' I said hotly. 'I'm fine.'

Jimmy held up his hands. 'Okay, okay, suit yourself.'

I softened. 'Well, there is something bothering me.'

Jimmy didn't say a word. He just watched me patiently.

'I've been feeling a bit funny.'

Stupid, I told myself. That wasn't it at all. I hadn't been feeling funny. I'd been passing out.

'You've got to take care of yourself,' Jimmy told me. 'You don't take risks with your health. I should know.'

'How do you mean?'

Jimmy patted his chest. 'It's the old ticker. Been giving me jip for a while.'

'Have you been to the doctor's?' I asked.

'Me? No. I've never had a day's sickness in my life. I don't like quacks.'

'Yes, but your heart ...'

'That's just it,' said Jimmy. 'It my heart and I'll take care of it in my own way. This'll do me just fine. Fifty lengths a day and I'm as fit as a fiddle.'

As if to prove his point, he pushed off from the side and started down the pool.

He was about half-way when it happened. I saw him rear up in the water, clutching his chest.

'Jimmy!' I cried.

I swam towards him. Why wasn't anybody else coming to his aid?'

'Jimmy!'

I reached him. He was threshing in the water, his eyes squeezed tight with pain.

'What is it?'

As his head went under he began to choke.

'Why doesn't somebody help him?' I cried.

The terrible hoarse roar of Jimmy's breathing mixed with a desperate gurgle as water filled his mouth and nose.

'Please.'

But the other swimmers were carrying on as if there was nothing out of the ordinary. In desperation I swam towards the grumpy lifeguard.

'Help me,' I pleaded. 'There's a man drowning.'

'Where?'

I turned to point, but the water where Jimmy had been fighting for his life was completely still. As for Jimmy, he had disappeared.

The superintendent handed me a can of Coke. I was sitting in his office, wrapped in a towel. The grumpy lifeguard nodded to his boss and left.

'But I'm not making it up,' I told the Superintendent. 'He was drowning. Some sort of heart attack.'

'And what was his name, this drowning man?'

'Jimmy Feeney.'

I saw a change in the Superintendent's expression.

'Come again.'

'Jimmy Feeney.'

'Is this a practical joke?'

'No, of course not. I know what I saw.'

'Mark tells me he's been watching you for weeks.'

'Mark?'

'The lifeguard who pulled you out of the pool. He said you were acting strangely, talking to yourself.'

'I was talking to Jimmy.'

'Jimmy Feeney, you mean?'

I nodded. What was it with him?

'Come with me?'

I followed the Superintendent down a corridor.

'Where are we going?'

'Haven't you been down here before?' he asked.

'No, why?'

'I thought you must have seen it.'

I was bewildered. 'Seen what?'

We were standing in front of a blue door. There was lettering on it: *Bootle and North Liverpool Swimming Club*. The Superintendent pointed to a plaque on the wall.

'I don't...'

And that's when I saw it.

This club room it read, *is dedicated to the memory of James Arthur Feeney. 1901–1967.*

'But it can't be,' I cried. 'I was talking to him a few minutes ago.'

'Either you're one of the world's best practical jokers,' said the Superintendent, 'Or else you've seen a ghost.'

My senses swam for a moment.

'Jimmy Feeney was a regular here,' the Superintendent explained. 'Never missed a day. But there was something he didn't know. He had this heart condition. It was like a time-bomb ticking away inside him, waiting to explode. What's sad is, a simple operation could have saved his life. But he was a proud man, stubborn even. He wouldn't go to the doctor's. It didn't matter how much his poor wife begged him, he just wouldn't go.'

'You knew him then?'

'Yes, he died during my first year here. I was a young lad then. We tried to save him, but he'd suffered a massive heart attack. He died on the way to hospital.'

I found myself sobbing.

'And he's just died again.'

The Superintendent rested his hand on my arm. 'Poor old Jimmy. So he's haunting the place. Funny that nobody's seen him before. I wonder why he chose you.'

I looked up into his face through my tears. Suddenly I knew why.

I told my mum that night. About the blackouts. She took me straight down to the hospital. After a couple more visits they told me I had epilepsy. I have fits. It's under control now, though. They gave me this medicine, Epilim. There are things I can't do, of course. Riding my bike's one. Swimming on my own is another. Except I don't. Swim on my own, I mean. Mum meets me there. I'm big mates with my grumpy lifeguard now. In fact, life's looking up in general. I seem to be able to handle the school bullies better. It's all down to Jimmy, of course. I can't forget what he did for me. It takes a big man to die twice so somebody else can live.

The Ghostagram

Gordon Snell

Emma and her twin brother Barry sat at the kitchen table doing their homework. Barry looked out of the window at their older sister Tracy, stretched out on a deckchair in the garden, sun-bathing.

'It's lucky for some!' said Barry.

'Yes, it's hard work being an actress!' said Emma.

Tracy's acting career since she left school had been a patchy one. She had had a couple of walk-on parts in television films, sung folk-songs in a pub, and done a radio commercial, playing a housewife going mad with delight at a new soap powder. But most of the time she did casual jobs, stacking supermarket shelves or working as a waitress in a local café.

Even when she was doing these jobs, she described herself as 'resting' between acting roles and so when Barry and Emma finished their homework and went to join Tracy in the garden, Emma said jokily, 'Still resting, Tracy?'

'Oh, you're a real comic, you are,' said Tracy pleasantly. 'But as a matter of fact I just landed a new job today.'

'A real acting part?' Barry was impressed. 'What as?'

'Oh, it could be all kinds of different characters, it depends what I'm asked to do.'

'Can we come and see you?' asked Emma.

'I'm afraid not, this is all for private functions, parties and such-like.'

'Are you a conjuror?' Barry wondered.

'Not exactly. I might be a glamour-girl one day, and a pink rabbit the next. There's even a gorilla costume. And I have to sing a special song each time. I'm what they call a Singing Telegram.'

'That sounds wonderful,' said Emma.

'Well, it will be good practice for acting different parts,' said Tracy, 'and it should be fun, being the surprise at a party.'

'Maybe you could come into our class as a gorilla and surprise Mrs Bagshaw?' Emma suggested. 'That would really be fun.'

'It sounds a bit dodgy.' said Tracy. 'Besides, I'd have to get paid.'

'No deal, then, I'm afraid,' said Barry.

But next day, they had an idea for a job they might hire Tracy to do. Mrs Bagshaw was droning on about the history of the Manor, a big mansion just outside the town. She was going to take the class to visit it next week.

'It sounds like Boresville,' whispered Emma.

'A yawn a minute with Baggy's Tours,' said Barry.

But then their friend Sue at the next desk decided to have a bit of fun. 'Has the Manor got a vampire, Mrs Bagshaw? I'll bring my wooden stake to stab it through the heart if you like.'

There was some giggling. Mrs Bagshaw looked stern, and said, 'I'm sorry to disappoint you, Susan, but no. No vampires. However, there is a fanciful story about a ghost. It's probably just made up, to attract more visitors.'

'Whose ghost is it?'

'Does it have a head?'

'Will we hear it scream?'

'Can you see through it?'

The questions came rattling out from the class. So Mrs Bagshaw told them the legend of the ghost.

'They call her The Woman in Green, and her name was Janie Lonquist. She is said to haunt the bedroom where her husband strangled her, two hundred years ago.'

'What did he do that for?' asked Emma.

'He had fallen in love with someone else, and he wanted to get rid of her.'

'The dirty rat!' said Sue. 'That's men all over!'

'Do you think we'll see her, Mrs Bagshaw?' asked Barry.

'Of course not, the ghost is only a story, even though it's true that Janie Lonquist disappeared and was never seen again.'

In the playground at break, they were acting out the story of Janie Lonquist, with Sue pretending to strangle Emma. After a long death scene with much gasping and groaning, Emma lay still.

Barry said in deep, mournful tones, 'And poor Janie Lonquist was never seen again ...'

'Until now!' said Emma, leaping to her feet and swooping around, moaning and rushing at people. Suddenly she stopped and said, 'That's a job for Tracy!'

'Your sister?' asked Sue.

'Right!' said Emma. She explained about Tracy's new job as a Singing Telegram. 'We'll take a collection round a few of us in the class, then we can hire Tracy, as a Ghostagram!'

At first, Tracy wasn't too sure if she liked the idea. She certainly doubted if the Singing Telegram firm would approve.

'You don't have to tell them,' said Barry. 'We'd be hiring you, on our own.'

'And the ghost of Janie Lonquist is a great part for an actress,' said Emma.

'You're right,' said Tracy, pleased. 'Okay, I'll do it. But I'll need to check out the scene first.'

'No problem,' said Barry. 'They have guided tours of the Manor every hour or so. We can go on one of those.'

On Saturday, Emma, Barry, Tracy and Sue queued up for the tour of the Manor. The guide first showed them the state rooms, the large drawing room with its ornate furniture and marble fireplace, and the dining room with a long polished table laid out for twenty people with fine china plates and silver cutlery.

'They knew how to live in those days,' said Sue.

'Those who managed to stay alive,' said Barry, 'unlike our friend Janie.'

'Now please follow me up the stairs,' said the guide.

They trooped up the wide oak staircase and along a corridor.

'This way,' said the guide, pushing open a heavy door.

The main bedroom was dark and gloomy. The walls were made of brown wood panels, and heavy velvet curtains were drawn across the windows. The guide pressed a switch, and a dim light with a velvet shade came on.

Against one wall they saw a huge four-poster bed, with a canopy over it, and deep red curtains hanging down the sides. The curtains on the far side of the bed were drawn across, but the ones near the group were drawn aside to show the wide bed, draped with a faded tapestry cover.

The guide described the furnishings, and then went on to tell the story of the murder of Janie Lonquist. The group listened with eager interest.

'Have you ever seen her ghost?' asked one of the visitors.

'Not personally,' said the guide, 'but there have been a number of sightings reported, and the Society for Psychical Research has shown great interest.'

Emma would love to have asked some questions, but they had all decided it was best to keep a low profile, so they wouldn't be remembered by any of the staff when the school group came and the haunting started.

When the guide led the group back out into the corridor to see the other upstairs rooms, the four of them stayed behind in the main bedroom. Quickly they went behind the drawn curtain on the far side of the bed.

'This is perfect,' said Tracy. 'I can hide behind this curtain, and pull it aside at the right moment, so they catch a glimpse of Janie.'

'And we'll all scream and point and generally go bananas,' said Sue.

'But how will you get into your costume, Tracy?' said

Barry. 'I know a way to do it!' said Tracy. I'll come on one of the official tours, the one before your school tour, and hide behind the curtain here till you arrive.'

'What about after you've appeared?' asked Barry. He believed in careful planning. Again they were baffled for a while. After all, some spoilsport no doubt would come looking behind the curtain for the ghost.

'I'll scramble under the bed,' said Tracy. 'They won't look there.'

'How about if I stand beside the light switch, and turn it out when you're ready to appear?' said Emma.

'Good idea,' said Sue. 'Hey, maybe there's a switch on this side of the room as well, which Tracy could use instead.'

She began to feel along the wooden panelling. She saw a small wooden knob and pressed it. Suddenly there was a creaking sound, and one of the panels near the floor slid open. They all stared in amazement. There was a hollow compartment behind the opening.

'The perfect hiding place!' Tracy exclaimed. 'I'm sure I can just squeeze in.' She put her head into the opening, and then crawled inside. There was a silence. The others gazed at the opening. Then suddenly, the panel slid shut.

Emma gasped. 'Tracy! Tracy!' she whispered, tapping on the wood. But there was no reply.

'She's walled up!' said Barry. 'We must get her out, or she'll suffocate.'

Then the panel opened again, and Tracy's head poked out. 'Hey, I had you fooled there, didn't I?' she said, grinning. They all laughed with relief, but the laughter was nervous and fearful.

Tracy scrambled out. 'I can hide in there after the haunting,' she said, 'and wait till your tour has gone. Then I'll change back into my ordinary gear, and just slip out and tag along with the next group.'

'Will you be able to breathe for that long?' Barry asked.

'Yes, the space is quite big inside,' said Tracy. 'But wow, it's dusty! And look what I found in a corner, on the floor.' She produced a piece of faded green silk.

Just then, they heard the voice of the tour guide outside, leading the group back the way they had come.

'Hurry, we'd better join on again before they notice we're missing,' said Tracy, stuffing the cloth in her pocket.

They hurried to the door, just in time to join the end of the shuffling group of visitors.

Back at home, they examined the silk scarf Tracy had found. It was a long scarf which had once had a pattern of flowers on it, picked out in gold thread.

'I'd say that cost a packet, once upon a time,' said Tracy.

'You could afford it if you were Lady Muck and married to the Lord of the Manor,' said Sue.

'Or if you were Janie Lonquist ...?' said Emma.

They all gazed at the scarf Tracy was holding. The story said Janie was strangled. Could this be the scarf she was wearing when it happened? The scarf her husband pulled tight around her throat, and then tighter and tighter?

'Her husband could have hidden it there, after he killed her,' Sue suggested.

'Perhaps he hid *her* there as well,' said Barry.

'A right barrel of fun *you* are,' said Tracy. 'But believe me, there was no skeleton in that cupboard. Only the scarf.'

'He probably moved her body later,' said Barry.

'Probably,' Tracy agreed with some sarcasm. 'I hope you're not trying to scare me out of this job you've offered me?'

'Well, I do wonder if it's such a good idea,' Barry said. 'It could be dangerous to mess about with the ... you know ...'

'The Other World?' said Emma in a spooky voice. 'Barry, you're not going to chicken out, are you?'

'We'd have to get rid of you then, wouldn't we?' said Sue. 'Still, you could always come back to haunt us as a headless chicken!'

Barry joined in the laughter, but he didn't sound very amused.

'Okay, so Operation Haunted House is on,' said Tracy. 'But I think I'll ask for payment in advance, just in case!'

They spent a lot of time going over the exact plan for the haunting. In Tracy's room they watched her try out her ghostly make-up. She tried green first of all, but it just made her look seasick. Then she tried for a skull-like effect, with black round her eyes, and some false teeth she had bought in a joke shop. Unfortunately, they just made her look goofy. Then she made up her face chalk-white, with dark hollows under the eyes, and purple lips.

'That's really scary!' said Emma. 'Try it with the torch.'

They drew the curtains and turned out the light. Tracy switched on a pencil torch and held it under her chin. She looked really spooky.

Emma asked Tracy, 'What are you going to wear?'

'I won't need a full costume,' said Tracy. 'It will be much more convincing if they just catch a glimpse of this ghastly face peeping through the curtains, and then it disappears again. I'll wear a green top, and a long black wig. With the make-up and the torchlight, that should do the trick.'

'You could always wear the scarf, too,' said Sue with a grin.

Tracy went a little pale. She looked at the seemingly harmless piece of cloth, lying on her dressing-table.

'I was only joking,' said Sue.

But Tracy felt she had been dared. 'It doesn't bother me,' she said. 'After all, it's probably not Janie's scarf at all – just one that somebody else threw away.'

None of them liked to wonder aloud why anyone would 'throw away' an old scarf in such an odd hiding place. But they were all thinking it.

'I'll wear it,' Tracy went on, jauntily. 'Here's to happy hauntings!' she said, draping the scarf around her neck.

On the day of the class tour, Tracy was packing her make-up bag when Emma and Barry came into her room.

'We got the money!' said Emma, producing an envelope with some notes and coins in it.

'The show had better be good,' said Barry, 'there's a lot of pocket money and piggy-bank savings in there.'

'You'll get value for money, don't you worry!' said Tracy.

As they travelled on the coach to The Manor, Mrs Bagshaw was pleased to notice the sense of excitement some of the children were showing. It was only a few of them admittedly; those twins and some of their friends, but they certainly seemed to be looking forward to the tour. Perhaps her teaching of history had really inspired them, for once.

Feeling that at last she had an interested audience, Mrs Bagshaw began to talk with a flourish and verve she rarely showed at school. In the downstairs state rooms, she described vividly the way of life of the people who had lived in these aristocratic houses – their riches, their fine furniture, the army of servants they had to wait on them.

Barry and Emma and their friends could hardly contain their impatience. When would Baggy stop rabbiting on and lead them upstairs? In the hallway they had seen the official tour finishing as they came in, and they knew that by now Tracy would be made up and waiting behind the curtain of the bed.

At last, they trooped up the stairs and along the corridor. Mrs Bagshaw opened the door of the main bedroom. There was a hush as the class went into the darkened room and stood about in the gloom. Emma felt as if her heart could have been heard beating, it seemed so loud.

Mrs Bagshaw turned on the light and began to talk about the bedroom and its furnishings, and how the curtains on the bed could be pulled to give privacy. For a moment Emma thought she wasn't going to refer to the ghost at all. But finally, almost as a postscript, she again told the story of Janie and how some people believed that her ghost haunted this very room.

Just then, Emma, who was standing near the switch, quickly reached over and turned it off. The room was plunged back into darkness. There were some gasps of surprise and alarm, and Mrs Bagshaw said, 'What happened?'

Then they heard a faint wailing moan, and the curtains at the far side of the bed were drawn aside just a little. In the gap could be seen a ghastly white face which seemed to glow in the darkness. It was the face of a young woman with long black hair, and her expression was one of silent, screaming horror. Round her neck she wore a green patterned scarf.

There were screams and cries of fright from everyone in the class. Some were actually cries of delight, as Emma and Barry and the people in the know, marvelled at how brilliantly Tracy had performed. Others, including Mrs Bagshaw's, were cries of real terror. Someone even fainted, and had to be picked up from the floor and revived.

The apparition lasted only a few seconds, then the curtains closed again and it disappeared.

Mrs Bagshaw gasped, 'Turn on the light! Turn on the

light!' Someone pressed the switch and the light came on. The room looked exactly as it had before.

No one seemed anxious to move. Then one of the bolder boys said, 'Let's catch it! Catch the ghost!' and rushed behind the curtain. He emerged again, looking puzzled. 'There's nothing here,' he said, pulling the curtains aside.

'Of course there isn't!' said Mrs Bagshaw, with great relief. She came and looked around at the scene behind the curtain. 'You see, it was all an illusion, some trick of the light, that's all. We just imagined we saw something.'

Emma smiled at Barry. They stole a glance at the wood panels of the wall, where they knew the 'ghost' of Janie Lonquist was hiding ...

Barry and Emma were waiting in the garden for Tracy to come home. An hour went by, then two hours.

'She should be home easily by now,' said Emma. 'The next tour was starting out just as our lot were leaving.'

'Maybe she stopped somewhere on the way home,' said Barry.

'But she said she'd come straight back so we could talk about it all.'

'You don't suppose the panel stuck and she couldn't get out?' wondered Emma.

'She said there was enough air in there, but she'll have been there much longer than we thought,' said Barry.

'The scarf!' Emma said in alarm. 'Perhaps it had a curse on it!'

'We must get back up to the Manor right away,' said Barry.

But just then, Tracy came out into the garden and met them.

'Listen, you two, I'm so sorry ...' she said.

'It's all right, we were just worried,' said Emma.

Tracy went on, 'I just hated to let you down, but there was nothing I could do. My boss at the firm rang not long after you left to get the coach to the Manor. It was an emergency. I had to fill in as a Singing Telegram at an office party. There was no way I could let you know. We'll do it another time, eh?'

'You mean you never went to the Manor?' said Emma in a shaky voice.

'No,' said Tracy, 'like I said, I got called out on this job.'

Emma and Barry looked at each other, wide-eyed with terror. If it wasn't Tracy they had seen in the bedroom, it must have been ...

'Is anything the matter?' asked Tracy. 'You both look as if you've seen a ghost!'

Mel and Squid and the Haunted Birds' Eggs

Douglas Hill

T he museum?' Mel said, amazed. 'Spend Saturday in the *museum*?'

'Not all day,' Squid said. 'Anyway, it could be a laugh.'

'What's funny about birds' eggs?' Mel asked.

'It's the *people* that would be funny,' Squid said. 'If there's a row about those stolen eggs.'

Mel thought about it. The local paper had mentioned the collection of eggs that had been left to the museum – embarrassingly, since it was against the law to take the eggs of most wild birds. It might be fun at that, she thought, to see what happens.

'All right,' she said. 'But if it gets boring, I'm not staying.'

They ambled away, looking a slightly mismatched pair. Mel, whose full name was Melanie, was a slim, dark-haired eleven-year-old; Squid, whose real name was Arthur, was a stocky redhead with round glasses, a few months younger than Mel and an inch or so shorter. Yet they were good friends as well as neighbours – partly because they had had some unusual adventures together.

Still, neither of them was expecting any sort of adventure at a *museum*. At least, not the town's Museum of Local History, which was on the top floor of the central library building. It displayed things from the town's past – and now it had a new exhibition, a gift from an old man named Caddon, who had died.

Mr Caddon had been a student of nature and a keen

collector. His collection held a few stuffed animals and birds, but mostly he had collected birds' eggs. Hundreds of them, from many kinds of birds in many countries.

And by taking those eggs, Mr Caddon had broken the law, time and again.

The paper had said that some people might go to the opening of the exhibition, that Saturday, to protest about showing the stolen eggs. So Mel and Squid were going to watch the fun.

When they got there, the 'fun' had already started. Going up the steps of the three-storey building that housed the central library and the museum, Mel and Squid could hear angry voices. When they went in, they saw a large crowd, all seeming to be talking at once.

And facing the crowd, with her library staff around her, was the head librarian, Miss Venter, a small pretty woman, looking oddly pale.

'This exhibition should *never* open!' a red-faced man was shouting. 'Every brat in this town will think it's all right to steal birds' eggs!'

'Perhaps,' Miss Venter replied, a bit shakily. 'But for the moment, the opening of the Caddon Collection has merely been postponed. Because of ...' she faltered, then went on, 'because of unforeseen events.'

As the hubbub went on, Mel and Squid moved to one side. 'So much for birds' eggs,' Mel muttered.

Squid scowled. 'Maybe not. Let's go upstairs and look around.'

Unnoticed, they drifted up the stairs to the next

floor. Then, with no one to stop them because everyone was downstairs in the hubbub, they kept going, up more stairs to the top floor.

There they found a small landing, and a closed door. Mel expected it to be locked, but when Squid turned the handle it opened easily, allowing them into the open-plan room where the museum was.

There was the Caddon Collection spread out before them.

The big room was dim and shadowy and totally silent. It was also oddly chilly, with a musty smell, as if it was in a deep cellar rather than on an upper floor. And all this, combined with the glittering glass eyes of the stuffed animals and birds, made Mel and Squid feel shivery.

Still, trying to ignore the eerie feeling, they gazed with awe at the huge expanse of birds' eggs, hundreds of them, set in trays with hand-written labels.

They were empty shells, of course, but their colours seemed as bright as if they were new-laid. Mel and Squid saw the glossy spotted eggs of larks, the soft blues and greys of thrush eggs, the olive-brown disguise of plover eggs, the speckled pink eggs of warblers, the startling brown-red of a nightingale's egg, the pale shiny almost-round eggs of owls ...

The collector, Mr Caddon, had taken eggs from nests all over the country, and from other countries as well. He had collected the eggs of game birds, seabirds, songbirds and birds of prey; eggs shaped like cylinders or cones; the tiny eggs of hummingbirds and wrens; the huge eggs of cranes and vultures ...

As Mel and Squid gazed and marvelled, a soft sound broke the silence around them.

Like the flap of a bird's wing.

They whirled, seeing nothing, but heard another flap, along with a scratchy rustling like claws on branches.

Again they saw nothing. Then Squid's elbow bumped a glass case holding a tiny stuffed pigmy shrew, and they suddenly heard a faint skittering on the floor, but still they saw nothing.

Then – with the room somehow growing even colder, even dimmer – they heard as if from far away the thin, haunting cry of a seabird.

And all at once, as if bursting into being from out of the chill dim emptiness of the air, the room was full of birds.

Flocks, swarms, blizzards of birds, of almost every sort and shape – hundreds upon hundreds of wings beating and thrashing and swooping. Hundreds of beaks open wide in wild outcry.

And every one of those birds was trying to fight its way through the feathered storm, in what looked like mindless fury, to get at Mel and Squid.

Gasping, they shrank away as the birds whirled down upon them – kestrels and peregrines, ravens and jays, swans and sandpipers, curlews and grebes. Dozens of other large birds, with clouds of smaller ones, woodpeckers and pipits, robins and swallows, swirling among them. Sharp beaks stabbed at Mel and Squid, hooked beaks and talons slashed at them, wings battered at them like clubs.

Yet as the attack went on – as they cried out in terror,

crouching, covering their heads – they became aware of an impossible thing.

They weren't being hurt – and there was almost no sound.

The dagger-beaks of hoopoes and kingfishers struck with no more power than grassblades. The tearing claws of barn owls and harriers brushed them as lightly as leaves. The huge wings of pelicans and storks fell on them as gently as feathers. And the raging cries from all those beaks were muffled and feeble, as if they were far away or behind plate glass.

As Mel and Squid peered up, astounded, they saw the reason. All of the birds wheeling and diving around them – and the few small furry creatures snapping around their feet – were misty, filmy, half-transparent shapes.

As if they were *ghosts* ...

Seeing that made the room seem even colder, the attack more terrifying. Moaning, Mel and Squid stumbled towards the door, while around them the ghostly birds kept up their furious, powerless attacks. Then at last the two of them plunged out of the big cold room, half-falling down the stairs.

No one in the library noticed them as they fled, white-faced, from the building. Hurtling away down the street as if they were being pursued, they stopped at last, out of breath, to huddle in a bus shelter.

'Mel,' Squid said, in a quavery voice. 'They were *ghosts*.'

Mel nodded shakily. 'You could see through them. And they were so *angry*!'

'As if they wanted to kill us,' Squid added. 'They

must be the ghosts of all the birds whose nests Mr Caddon robbed ... all the birds who lost their eggs ...'

Mel nodded again. 'I wonder if they attacked Mr Caddon like that ...' She stopped, with a gasp. 'I wonder if they attacked the *librarians*!'

Squid went wide-eyed. 'That could be why Miss Venter looked so pale – and why she wouldn't open the exhibition!'

Mel sighed. 'Poor sad bird-ghosts ... and the little animal-ghosts too.'

'They're probably doomed to haunt the collection forever,' Squid whispered.

They thought about that as they moved away, trying to put the memory of terror behind them.

'Aren't there supposed to be ways,' Mel said at last, 'that ghosts can be set free, somehow? So they don't have to go on haunting?'

'I think there are,' Squid said. 'I've read that some-where.' He peered at her. 'Are you thinking about *doing* something? *Helping* the ghosts?'

'Maybe,' Mel said. '*Someone* should help them. And it's not as if they hurt us ...'

They went on thinking about it until at last they parted to go home. And through that day and the next, they kept thinking about it. About the sadness of it all, and the unfairness – how one selfish old egg-thief had forced hundreds of birds into that frenzied haunting, without hope of rest or peace.

Then, on Sunday evening, Squid phoned Mel.

'I've found a way to put ghosts to rest, in a ghost story!' he said excitedly. 'You just scatter *salt* and *garlic*

– like with vampires – and speak a spell, and the ghost never walks again!'

'What spell?' Mel asked.

'It goes like this,' Squid said. 'Depart from this place, unquiet spirit, to thy longed-for rest, and come no more.'

Mel frowned. 'It doesn't sound like much. And it's just in a story.'

'It might work, though,' Squid said. 'It's worth a try.'

So they agreed. They would go back to the museum the next day, after school, with salt, garlic and the spell, and try.

They felt quite nervous going into the library the next afternoon, pockets bulging with salt and garlic. But no one noticed as they went up the stairs, so they were alone as they reached the top floor and entered the museum again, shivering in the chill dimness.

Quickly they brought out the containers of salt and began scattering it over the floor. And they kept grimly on – glancing around nervously – when they heard the first muffled flap of wings, faint rustlings, then the distant hoot of an owl.

Suddenly the room went icy-cold as before, and the bird-ghosts appeared, in the same whirling tornado of fury, hurtling down upon the two of them.

But with a difference – as Squid was first to find out.

'Ow!' he yelled. 'That hurt!'

He stared at his hand, where a ghostly beak had jabbed him – and where a trickle of blood was showing. By then, Mel had felt a heavy thump from a wing, a sharp tug of claws in her hair. And the screams and whistles and cries of the birds were far louder than before.

'They're stronger!' she cried. 'More *solid*!'

She flung up her arms as a group of sharp-beaked sea-birds flashed down at her and gasped as she felt a sharp nip on her ankle from the tiny ghost of the pigmy shrew. The pain wasn't much worse than a stab from a rose-thorn – but if the ghosts went on getting *more* solid …

They'll tear us to bits, Mel thought in near-panic.

'Come on!' she cried – and they ran for the door, while the bird-ghosts continued their ferocious, painful attacks. Leaping out of the museum and slamming the door, they stood shivering with shock.

'How could they have got more solid?' Squid asked wildly.

'No idea,' Mel muttered. 'They weren't bothered by the salt, either.'

'It's not supposed to work on its own,' Squid reminded her. 'It needs garlic and that spell.'

Mel blinked unhappily. 'So we have to go back in.'

'But maybe we shouldn't stay so long,' Squid suggested. 'It takes the ghosts a while to appear, every time – so we could just go in for a minute, then duck out again before they arrive.'

'Good idea,' Mel said, encouraged.

Nervously, they opened the door, to see that the bird-ghosts had vanished again. Rushing in, they pulled garlic bulbs from their pockets, separated the cloves and scattered them around with the salt, while hearing the first flapping and rustling around them.

Then they dashed for the door, just before the bird-ghosts reappeared in their tempest of fury. And though a buzzard's wing nearly knocked Squid over, and a falcon's beak ripped Mel's sleeve, they got out unharmed.

'I hope that spell works,' Mel panted, on the landing. 'It's getting dangerous in there.'

They waited edgily for a moment or two, then went in again, salt and garlic crunching under their shoes. Squid brought out a paper with the spell on it and began to read: 'Depart from this place, unquiet spirits ...'

Again, while he read, the warning bird-sounds began – louder than ever, Mel thought. And when Squid finished, and they were hurrying to the door, the room seemed to grow silent, as if the spell had worked.

But then they heard brisk footsteps outside the door, and a key turning in the keyhole. Locking them in.

Just as the raging storm of birds reappeared in the air around them.

'Help!' they screamed, banging wildly on the door. 'Let us out! Help!'

But they could hear nothing beyond the door, over the deafening noise of the ghosts. And they had to stop banging on the door to cover their heads with their arms, cowering, while beaks and claws raked and stabbed and slashed at them with fearful, *solid* strength. Screaming in pain and terror, they were being overpowered by that endless, maddened, attack.

And then the door was jerked open, and they half-fell through it. The noise of the ghosts cut off as the door slammed shut again – and in the sudden quiet they found themselves face to face with Miss Venter.

She looked as shocked as they did. 'I'm sorry, I had no idea anyone was in there. Whatever happened?'

'We ... er ... the eggs ...' Squid stammered.

'The eggs are *haunted*,' Mel said, gathering herself. 'And we wanted ... to help the bird-ghosts.'

'So you saw them, too,' murmured Miss Venter. And she told them that when she and her assistant were setting up the exhibition, the bird-ghosts had appeared and attacked them – which was why she had cancelled the opening.

'But we could only *see* the misty ghosts,' she went on. 'We *felt* nothing. We weren't harmed, as you two have been.'

Mel and Squid looked at each other. They both looked as if they had been dragged through a prickly hedge – their clothes torn, scratches and bruises on their hands and arms and faces.

'They're not misty now,' Mel said. 'They've been getting more solid, each time they appear.'

'They're really dangerous,' Squid added.

Miss Venter shivered. 'Something has to be done.' She peered at them. 'What did you mean about trying to *help* the ghosts?'

Squid explained about the spell, which they had thought might stop the haunting. And Miss Venter nodded thoughtfully.

'It was a good idea,' she said, 'even if it didn't work. And you were very brave.' She paused, thinking. 'It's very strange that they should be getting solid only *now*, here in the museum. You'd think they would have become solid long before this – by appearing to Mr Caddon, when the collection was still in his house!'

'Maybe he had some way to stop them,' Mel suggested.

Miss Venter nodded – and then went very still, her eyes wide. 'That's *it*,' she breathed. 'Mr Caddon's cousin, who brought us the collection, did say that it was a bit musty – because it had been kept in the *basement*.'

Mel blinked. 'How would that help?'

'Because,' Miss Venter said, smiling, 'long ago, people believed that a ghost can be laid to rest simply by giving the person's body a proper burial.'

Squid frowned. 'Are you saying the eggshells should be buried?'

Mel's eyes lit up. 'No! She means they could be put back in a basement. Just as if they *were* buried! Like a sort of tomb!'

'Exactly,' Miss Venter said. 'And the library has an excellent basement, with a storeroom. The ghosts might disappear completely, if we put the collection down there.'

Mel and Squid twitched. 'Wait, wait,' Mel said quickly. '*We*?'

'There's no one else I can ask,' Miss Venter said. 'And if we do what you were doing – rush in for a load of eggs and out again before the birds appear – there should be no danger.'

'They could come after us, on the stairs!' Mel said, thinking of all the trips to and from the basement, carrying trays of eggs, while bird-ghosts shrieked and slashed around them.

'There's a small lift,' Miss Venter said, 'for carrying heavy loads of books. And if things do get dangerous, we'll stop at once. But you did say you wanted to help the ghosts ...'

So Mel and Squid agreed, a bit unhappily. And the work began.

Twilight was falling by then, adding to the feeling of spookiness as Miss Venter put on a heavy smock, and found sturdy work-gloves for them all. Then they took deep breaths and rushed into the museum. Quickly they each stacked up several trays of eggs, which fitted neatly on top of one another, then hurried towards the door of the lift, on the far wall.

But the lift ground its way towards them with agonising slowness. And in that time the ghostly bird-sounds began – until, with a hawk's shrill scream, the bird-ghosts burst into view once more, in another shrieking, blood-thirsty attack.

But just in time the lift door slid open, and the three of them leaped in with their burdens, so that only one beak jabbed Mel's shoulder, only one claw scraped Miss Venter's smock. On the way down they heard eerie rustlings, but no ghosts had appeared in the lift by the time they reached the dank gloom of the basement.

And as they carried the trays into the storeroom, even the weird bird-sounds vanished.

'I think it's going to work,' Squid said softly.

On the next trip, they gathered more trays of eggs as quickly as before, and this time the lift was waiting on the top floor. But on the way a flock of bird-ghosts did invade the lift, snapping and clawing. Still, their more solid wings were cramped inside the lift, and their attacks were blocked by the stacked trays that Mel and Squid and Miss Venter were holding in gloved hands.

And when the lift reached the basement, the flock of ghosts also vanished.

'It really *is* working!' Mel said with relief.

Encouraged, they carried on – working swiftly, facing only brief, limited attacks in the lift on each trip. Until finally, when they went up to the museum for the very last trays of eggs, only a handful of bird-ghosts came to threaten them. And those, too, vanished when they reached the basement.

So all the eggs, along with the stuffed animals and birds, had been moved safely down to the storeroom – and there were no ghosts to be seen, anywhere.

'We did it!' Squid cried.

Mel nodded, sighing. 'They're all at peace, now.'

'I'm terribly grateful to you both,' Miss Venter said. 'And I think the collection can just stay here, until everyone has forgotten …'

She stopped, with a small shriek, as something tiny and furry skittered across the floor.

'Just a mouse,' Squid said, laughing, as they turned towards the door.

But if they had looked closely, they would have seen that the small furry thing looked exactly like the stuffed pigmy shrew, in its glass case. They would also have seen it skitter on – growing mistier, as it went – until it came to the wall and went right on *through* it, without stopping. Before vanishing entirely, forever.

dolphin story collections

chosen by Wendy Cooling

1 top secret
stories to keep you guessing by Rachel Anderson, Andrew Matthews, Jean Richardson, Leon Rosselson, Hazel Townson and Jean Ure

2 on the run
stories of growing up by Melvin Burgess, Josephine Feeney, Alan Gibbons, Kate Petty, Chris Powling and Sue Vyner

3 aliens to earth
stories of strange visitors by Eric Brown, Douglas Hill, Helen Johnson, Hazel Townson and Sue Welford

4 go for goal
soccer stories by Alan Brown, Alan Durant, Alan Gibbons, Michael Hardcastle and Alan MacDonald

5 wild and free
animal stories by Rachel Anderson, Geoffrey Malone, Elizabeth Pewsey, Diana Pullein-Thompson, Mary Rayner and Gordon Snell

6 weird and wonderful
stories of the unexpected by Richard Brassey, John Gatehouse, Adèle Geras, Alison Leonard, Helen McCann and Hazel Townson

7 timewatch
stories of past and future by Stephen Bowkett, Paul Bright, Alan MacDonald, Jean Richardson, Francesca Simon and Valerie Thame

8 stars in your eyes
stories of hopes and dreams by Karen Hayes, Geraldine Kaye, Jill Parkin, Jean Richardson and Jean Ure

9 spine chillers
ghost stories by Angela Bull, Marjorie Darke, Mal Lewis Jones, Roger Stevens, Hazel Townson and John West

10 bad dreams
horror stories by Angela Bull, John Gatehouse, Ann Halam, Colin Pearce, Jean Richardson and Sebastian Vince

11 it's christmas
stories about Christmas by Mary Hoffman, Geraldine McCaughrean, Kate Petty, Alison Prince and Jean Richardson

12 ride like the wind
horse stories by Jane Ayres, Linda Jennings, Pamela Kavanagh, Christine Pullein-Thompson and Lorna Read

13 side splitters
stories to make you laugh by Elizabeth Dale, Ann Jungman, Alex Shearer, Ruth Symes and Nick Turnbull

14 out of this world
stories of virtual reality by Malorie Blackman, Eric Brown, Nick Gifford, Rhiannon Lassiter and Lorna Read

15 dare you
stories to surprise you by Eric Brown, Mary Hoffman, Mary Hooper, Leon Rosselson and Ruth Symes

16 we are champions
soccer stories by William Crouch, Peter Dixon, Alan Durant, Alan Gibbons and Sam Jackson

17 simply spooky
ghost stories by Annie Dalton, Alan Gibbons, Douglas Hill, Chris Powling and Gordon Snell

18 stranger than ever
mysterious stories by Annie Campling, Simon Edge, Nick Gifford, Hazel Townson and Susannah White

19 surprise surprise
stories to make you wonder by Simon Edge, Sue Inman, Caroline Pitcher, Kathy Still and Nicholas Walker

20 scared stiff
horror stories by Jane Ayres, Alan Durant, Catherine Fisher, Kenneth Ireland and Jean Richardson